MURDER
PREMONITIONS

MURDER
PREMONITIONS

Nubian Star

Table of Contents

Veronica 8

Gina 10

Derek 12

Gina 14

Veronica 16

Derek 19

Gina 20

Naomi 22

Gina 25

Derek 26

Veronica 29

Gina 30

Neil 33

Carrie 37

Neil 41

Derek 45

Lopez 47

Neil 52

Vince 54

Gina 56

Derek 58

Gina 60

Veronica 69

Derek 70

Neil 72

Epilogue 78

Gina 78

About the Author 81

"There are some people—people the universe seems to have singled out for special destinies. Special favours and special torments. God knows we're all drawn towards what's beautiful and what's broken: I have been, but some people cannot be fixed. Or if they can be: it's only by love and sacrifice so great that it destroys the giver."

- Cassandra Clare

Veronica

I walked out of the doors of Nordstrom like it was a runway during New York Fashion Week. Being a bronzed blonde who is five-feet-eight with well-toned legs, a 24" waist and size 42DD bust, packaged in this season's latest Marc Jacobs fashion, I looked like a model. I felt like a million bucks, and with the amount of shopping bags I was carrying, it looked like I tried to spend the same amount. As I put my $700 Gucci Butterfly sunglasses over my eyes, I sidestepped a group of gothic teenage girls—with horribly pale skin and even worse black makeup—complaining about Emos.

I had no idea what that meant, but from their high-pitch crescendos of different agreements, I could tell that being an "Emo" wasn't cool. Listening to the girls complain, I thought about my days in high school as I scanned the parking lot for my car. As I spotted my silver Mercedes SLC300, I cursed Tom, my trainer, because I listened to him today; I parked at the far end of the parking lot to get in my steps for the day. Even though the practice had a real impact on the firmness of my glutes, it wasn't enjoyable taking so many steps on asphalt in 6" Valentino Garavani pumps with my arms laden with heavy bags.

Trying to take my mind off the pain in the arch of my feet with every step, I started writing my mental *To-Do List* of things I needed to get done before the dinner party that night. I needed to call the caterer to let them know that six more people would be joining the party and make sure the gardener would be finished before 3 PM. I was so distracted with my thoughts that I didn't see the beat-up Dodge Caravan with plastic tarp and duct tape for a back window until its bumper was almost touching my bags.

"Hey!" I yelled loudly, causing the driver to slam on his brakes.

An overweight middle-aged man with three chins and a dirty blond balding mullet poked his portly head out of the driver's side window, "Watch where you're walking, I'm trying to back up here! You're going to get that skinny ass of yours hit!"

Unable to contain my anger at such a rude response, I yelled back, "Maybe if you actually LOOK before you back up, you wouldn't have almost run over somebody!" Before he could say anything else, I walked off. The audacity of people never ceased to amaze me! I walked the rest of the way to my car, unable to stop the mental rant that was blaring in my head. I just didn't understand how people can be so cruel to one another.

I arrived at the back of my Benz and realize that I didn't get out my keys to unlock the car. If it hadn't been for that fat balding mullet man, I wouldn't have been so distracted. As I fumbled in my cavernous purse for my keys, I placed my shopping bags on the ground. *I really need to clean out this purse*, I thought as I continued to search. When I finally found them, I popped the trunk.

Looking down at all the bags clustered around my feet, I was oblivious to everything else that was going on around me. I picked up the biggest bags first to put them in the back of the trunk, for the SLC300, being a two-seater, had an extremely deep trunk. It was one of the reasons I chose it, that and the fact that I looked so amazing behind the wheel. I smiled as I reached for another set of bags. Before it even registered in my brain what was happening, my feet were lifting off the ground.

This was the first time all day I felt some relief in my aching feet, but I still couldn't understand why. Confused, I tried to turn my body but couldn't. There were large hairy arms in a denim sleeves with a vice grip around my waist. An overpoweringly strong chemical smell filled my nose as I feel something cold and wet cover my face, and the last thing I remembered was the feeling of being pulled backward. Then everything went black.

Gina

I gasped as I sat up in my bed with a jolt, clawing at my chest. I could still feel the intensely crushing weight of his arm around me. The high-pitched buzzing of my alarm clock made the walls of my bedroom pulse simultaneously with my heart. Foggy from the deep sleep and strange dream that was fighting to hold onto me, I was confused and disoriented. The alarm clock's buzz drilling into my brain made it harder to catch my bearings. I willed my alarm clock to stop the awful buzzing, but it didn't work, the neon red digital numbers shook the fog from my mind. It was 7:25 a.m.

"Shit, I'm late!" Frantically, I threw back the covers and jumped from my bed in a hurried run to the bathroom. I had to be at work in 35 minutes and it would take me at least 30 to get there in minimal traffic! "How did I oversleep again?" I screamed to no one as I scrambled from my closet to the bathroom and back again. Normally, I would just call Prescott and Kramer Securities and let my assistant know I was running late. As a managing logistical analyst in an up and coming private securities firm, I had that luxury. But today I was supposed to give a presentation to upper management. This would be a make or break presentation to get that corner office if it all went well; but I could easily be bumped down if I blew it.

My obsessive need for perfection actually worked in my favour, because I had laid my underwear, suit, and bag out before I went to bed last night. I worked out the routes I could take in my head as I rushed in, buttoning up my lucky periwinkle blue silk blouse. I literally hopped my way to the front door, putting on my navy-blue slacks on the way and slipping on my favourite black Pumas. *I will put on my pumps once I get to the office.*

I jumped into my black 2002 Honda Civic, panting as I slammed the key into the ignition—27 minutes to get there. *A Tribe Called Quest* came on in a decibel much too loud for that time of the morning. I turned the radio off. I knew I needed to get my thoughts together for the presentation, but I was feeling off. As I made it to the corner of my block to make the turn to get to the freeway, I tried to pin down the feelings of foreboding. I couldn't quite shake that strange dream off, but I had to get my head in the game. Going over the speech in my head, I focus on my delivery during the PowerPoint presentation. I need to speak slowly enough that they clearly hear my ideas but come across exciting and engaging too. I've seen way too many people in my position bore the Bigwigs and watch their chances for advancement get snatched away.

Snatched. Isn't that what happened in that dream? I had dreamt about a woman getting kidnapped. Where in the hell did that even come from? It was strange because I fell asleep watching Animal Planet; I didn't watch anything else, and I hadn't listened to a True Crime podcast in more than two weeks. I shook my head in an attempt to regain my focus; I needed to remember the numbers for the middle of the presentation. I had 17 minutes to get there and I was just making it on to the freeway, cursing loudly. I knew from the long lines of cars, without a pardon from God, I wouldn't be there on time. I picked up my cell and hit one key on the speed dial, the voice of my assistant Wendy came on the line after two rings.

"Ms. Porter's office, how may I assist you?"

"Wendy, I'm running late! Traffic is a bitch and it's going to be at least 25-30 minutes before I get there. Have the board members arrived yet?"

"No, I just spoke to Mr. Higgin's admin and the board members had to take a slight detour this morning before the presentation; they rescheduled it for 10 AM."

"Thank Sweet Baby Jesus! Okay, I'll be there as soon as the traffic permits. Please order my breakfast and have a huge cup of Earl Gray waiting."

Wendy clicked off the line. I sat back saying a small prayer of thanks for the pardon, clicked the radio back on, enjoying the blare of *A Tribe Called Quest* with a smile.

Derek

I sat at the dinner table, not really paying attention to what my wife, Carrie, was saying. It was becoming harder and harder to stay present with her, with the whole family really. Life with a wife and five kids was getting boring, and now that she was pregnant again, it felt like the walls were starting to close in. It wasn't always like this. In the beginning, it used to be fun. When I met Carrie in college, at the beginning of sophomore year, she stood out. Most people bore me with their basic intellects and mundane lives, but she was different. She was extremely efficient, very intelligent, yet down to earth enough to not need to flaunt it. She had a light sense of humour, and she had my train of thought, which was a bullet train compared to the average. I'd never even entertained the idea of a girlfriend before meeting Carrie, but after spending time with her, it seemed like the most logical thing. It was an added bonus that she was attractive. She was not the epitome of beauty by social norms, but she had a natural beauty about her. At only five feet tall, she was petite. She had sunburned brunette hair and a small round face, with almond-shaped eyes the colour of warm chestnut. Her nose was what would be referred to as a button nose and she had soft, pouty, rosy, pink lips. When she smiled, her entire face lit up. Being with Carrie was unlike any other time in my life. She made me laugh, she challenged my thoughts intellectually and socially, and she had a way of showing the world to me from a totally different lens. She showed me what it would be like if I felt emotions.

Now, fifteen years and five and a half kids later, she was a frumpy nag who only talked about kids' activities, household chores, bills, and, more specifically, about me making the money to pay all said bills. We'd both worked after graduation, but as soon as Thaddeus was born, Carrie never went back to work in any full-time capacity. She'd start working, but soon after, we would discover she was pregnant, and there came another year and a half of me providing the sole income.

One of the things that I had really liked about her when I met her was her independence. But now, she was just like any other Susie from Middle America hoping for a knight in shining armour while staying at home with her own homegrown nursery of kids. I consented to the first two pregnancies to do what I thought was my husbandly duty as per social norm. I knew that with the demands of my job, Carrie would have to deal with the majority of the parental work. I also knew I could fake my way through the times I did have to engage with them and I could still have time to get out and do what I needed to take the edge off. We were scientifically strategic as the boy and girl she wanted were conceived in the first two pregnancies. I thought we were done, but her maternal clock had other plans. The other three and a half kids came out of Carrie's nagging insistence.

Sitting at the table with Carrie and all of the kids, half-listening to her go on about some PTA mom she didn't like, pretending to eat Tuesday's dinner of meatloaf, mashed potatoes, and green beans, I felt like a giant in a clown car. I needed to get out of there and go back to the one place I felt truly comfortable, where I was king! Where *she* was waiting for me. She had been sleeping for about six hours now; I had another three before she woke up. I wanted to get things set up for our first time playing together. My member jumped a bit at the thought. I held back a smile because I hadn't felt this kind of excitement since the last one, but she expired too quickly. She wasn't the right type, anyway; this new one was perfect!

Unable to contain myself, I put down my fork, wiped my mouth with my napkin although I hadn't really eaten any of Carrie's dry Tuesday Meatloaf, stood up at the table, announced I would be back later, and walked away before any of them could say differently. By the time the sound of Carrie's annoying voice hit my ears, I was closing the front door. I knew when I came home I would have to deal with what I had just done, but I didn't care. It was time to play.

Gina

Making the closing statement, I knew I had killed it! I made an impact with my discoveries and projections, and the dollar signs that were dancing in the eyes of the bosses at the table confirmed it. Immediately after the meeting, I was told to get on the schedule of the VP of Logistics' calendar for next week. That corner office just might soon officially be mine!

When I got back to my office, I closed my door and blinds to have a moment to myself. I quietly broke out in a victory dance as the feeling of accomplishment washed over me. I had worked so hard to get to this position in a company that wasn't known for promoting brown faces. I was on the fast track to becoming the youngest member of upper management. Even though the day had started off wrong with oversleeping and that crazy dream, things had aligned correctly, and I would be meeting with Mr. Prescott next week!

Once I stopped my little internal party, I checked my calendar to see what was scheduled for the rest of my day. Since I didn't have another meeting for another 30 minutes, I decided to get a light snack. One of the perks of working at Prescott and Kramer Securities was that all meals, snacks, and beverages were provided by the company. There was a five-star restaurant quality "cafeteria" where you could get anything from fresh organically grown fruit to gluten-free paninis. There were gourmet coffees and hand-rolled teas, freshly baked goods, and a deli. Prescott and Kramer took the perks and benefits to another level.

As I sat down at a table to eat the bowl of organic pineapple from the fruit bar, the flat screen on the wall in front of me caught my attention.

"BREAKING NEWS: We have just received reports that 25-year-old Social Media personality, Veronica Bridges, is missing. She was last seen shopping at Bayshore Mall yesterday. However, it is unclear what happened to her once she left the mall. When she didn't show up for her own annual fundraiser dinner party, authorities were notified. The police have not released any statements at this time. We reached out to both Ms. Bridges' publicist and family but have received no response. If you have any information regarding the whereabouts of Ms. Veronica Bridges, please contact authorities immediately! Back to you, Ken."

I choked on the pineapple I was chewing as the picture of Veronica Bridges filled the forty-two inches screen. The face that filled the screen was a young blonde with baby blue eyes. My heart pounded in my chest in an instant. I coughed, making sure I didn't choke.

Veronica

The strong scent of mint filled my nose as I felt the moist heat of his breath on my cheek. My eyelids felt glued together as I struggled to open them but couldn't. Even if I could, there was something covering my eyes. *Where am I? What's happening?* The smell of mint was overpowering, and I felt the dizziness grab hold of me viciously. I felt the bile rise up in my throat, pushing its way out of my mouth. Instinctively, I tried to lift my body to project the vomit away from me, but immediately, I found that I could not move my limbs. Suddenly, strong fingers turned my head to the left, as the bile erupted from my mouth.

The memories of shopping at Nordstrom came flooding back to me: The beat-up minivan and the tripled chinned fat man with the dirty balding mullet, the fumbling for my keys, and the vice grip on my stomach. It all came flooding back like scenery on a whirl-a-wheel at the carnival. Was it the fat mullet man who had me? It couldn't be. I didn't remember feeling a stomach when that arm grabbed me. I retched again as the reality of what happened to me began to sink in. The strong hand held my hair. My mind began to register all the things that were possibly going to happen to me as my heartbeat doubled with that understanding. I felt my body burst out in a sweat, but I wasn't sure if it was from the vomiting or the fear that was now coursing through me. I felt moist heat crawling up the side of my neck, hovering at my left earlobe. He kissed me softly and I cringed.

"It's okay, Veronica."

I stifled a cry that was trying to escape.

"I know this is all very disorientating, waking up like this in a strange place, feeling dizzy. Ah...I hate that it had to be this way, but we both know you like a certain type and let's just say... I'm not him. So, I decided to stack the odds in my favour and just take you. Let me tell you right now that you can't get away. No one can find you. You are mine now, and you will do what I say," he added.

I cringed imagining the smirk he now wore with pride.

"But let's not worry about all the formalities. We have all night to get acquainted..." His rough hand brushed against my cheek and I pulled back. He laughed at that. It was a guttural laugh. "I think you're going to like what I have in store for you. I apologize for the sickness but sometimes people have a severe reaction to chloroform, even if you think you've calculated the height and weight perfectly." He went quite. "Did you eat this morning before you went shopping, dear?"

The concern in his voice seemed genuine but it irked me.

"You probably didn't. I know you're not really a breakfast person. Did you go jogging that 5K without taking your water bottle again? You know Tom would tell you that dehydration is the devil. Well, never mind all that."

There was a long pause followed by footsteps, ones that lead away from me. I tried to move but it was no use. Just as quickly as he had walked away, he was next to me again. "Let's play," he said, menacingly.

As I felt him begin to cut the clothes from my body, my mind reeled at what he'd just said to me. He knew that I didn't eat breakfast, that I jogged 5K every other morning, and my trainer's name was Tom. He even knew how Tom spoke to me! My mind began to fracture as I tried to understand how he could possibly know all these things about me! I felt instantly cold as he cut my underwear from my body. For the first time in my life, I didn't want to be the object of a man's attention. Even though I couldn't see him, I could feel his eyes all over me like I was covered by a swarm of ants. I tried to move, but whatever he had me bound with cut tighter into my skin.

"What do you want from me? How long have I been here?" I managed to get out in a strained whisper.

He didn't verbally answer but touched the left side of my stomach. I tried to recoil from the feel of his fingers on my body, but again, the bindings tightened. My panting breath caught in my chest from the squeeze of what felt like ropes. I could feel that he was standing close. The heat that was coming from his body was almost visible, even though I couldn't see it, I sensed it. I could smell the overpowering scent of mint again as I felt him kiss the side of my neck. Tears began to stream from the corners of my eyes, as his tongue flicked the nipple of my left breast. A cry escaped my lips as he took the entire nipple in his mouth and bit down hard. I felt the warmth of my blood run down my side, as he chuckled lightly.

"You taste as good as I thought you would!" he said, biting down on me again.

The pain of his teeth tearing into my skin was blaring hot as if I was being ripped open by a heated hook. My screams echoed in my ears like they didn't belong to me. I felt the cold point of a knife drag slowly down the right side of my chest, and then I howled in pain.

Derek

"Oh, Veronica, you don't know how long I have been waiting to have this moment with you! I have suffered for too long having to pretend to be normal, to be weak like everyone else. I have watched you for months. I know all your routines. You were so easy to learn," I said as I slashed the pink flesh above her right hip with the serrated tip of my KA-BAR knife.

My manhood stood pulsing at the sight of Veronica's roped and blood-covered body. My entire body vibrated with pleasure. I hadn't experienced this level of arousal in so long and I felt like I could explode. For the last six years, I've tried to hold it in. I tried to pretend Carrie was someone else, but every time I touched her, she became pregnant. *I hate her pregnant body. So disgustingly normal. She's nothing more than a dog, breeding every time she's in heat.* Her body used to be so tight, toned, like the body I'm now playing with. But now, she was flabby and filled with stretchmarks. Ugh! I can't believe I was even able to keep an erection! If it wasn't for the trophies I had from the last girl, I never would have been able to do it.

It had been two days since I'd had Veronica. Unable to contain myself any further, I angled the table to enter her. Feeling the warmth of her insides, I thrust into her ferociously, pumping away six years of disgust and regret. Every time I entered her, it replaced a memory of Carrie's vile body and excited me more. Her screams intensified and sent me into a frenzy; I bit down on her shoulder. Feeling my climax approaching, I drove deeper into her, encouraged by the resistance of her body. The sound of my heartbeat drowned out her screams as I emptied my seed into her. Collapsing on top of Veronica, I thought to myself, *She was better than I imagined.*

Gina

The sound of my own screams reverberated off the walls of my bedroom, like the bouncing balls I played with as a child. My pillowcase was soaked from the tears that stained my face and I could still feel the knife piercing my skin. Sitting up, I lowered the right side of my pyjama pants to see if there was a cut there. The dream. I grabbed my head as it registered to me that I was checking for a cut that I had received in the nightmare I was just having. But I wasn't me in the dream; I was that missing girl.

Why was I dreaming about this missing girl? *That news story is getting to me*, I told myself internally, but quickly remembered that I'd seen her in my dream before the news. This didn't make sense. The dream was so vivid. I *was* Veronica; everything she experienced, I experienced. We were being tortured by some freak that chewed raw mint leaves and hated his nagging wife. I could feel and hear everything she felt and heard. It was the same with him too. But how could that be? I sat back on my headboard and pulled my knee to my chest. As I pulled the covers around me, I felt a shock go through my spine and I had flashes of a memory that I couldn't make out. I was still feeling the places he bit her, the places he cut her, on my own body!

He had been so excited to hear her scream, to see her blood spill from her body. It was the sickest thing I had ever experienced in my life! I jumped up with a jolt and I almost didn't make it to the small wastebasket in the corner of my bedroom before the bile flew from my lips. Sitting on the floor of my bedroom, spitting the last of the acid from my churning stomach into the basket, I tried to make sense of what was happening to me. I was somehow dreaming about a girl who was now missing, and if my latest dream was correct, she was being raped and tortured now, too.

But how could that be? How could I be dreaming about a missing girl that I didn't even know existed before I had seen her on the news?

The rational part of my brain struggled to make sense of this information. Something inside of me felt there was something there, but I didn't know what. Was my subconscious playing tricks on me? Getting off the floor, I slowly made my way to the bathroom, turned on the faucet, and splashed cold water on my face. I stared at my reflection, and again, I tried to make sense of what was happening.

I always had a strong intuition. Even as a kid, the phone would ring and I would just know who was on the other line before anyone answered. I always knew when someone had died or was dying. There was a feeling that would come over me. It was like lightning pulsing through my brain. My grandma used to say it's because I had "the sight." She would always say I was "special" like she was.

It was like she knew everything! She knew when things had happened without anyone telling her. People in the neighbourhood would come see her for advice and she was always right. I remember games we would play, where she would hide things and see if I could find them. She would ask me what colour or number she was thinking of. I guessed right most of the time, but when I didn't, it really made me feel like there was nothing special about me. My grandma died when I was seven years old; I didn't know it was going to happen. I was so angry that my specialness didn't save my grandma. I stopped believing I was special, but my gut was usually right 98% of the time. I just felt vibes about things. I would have feelings about things and people, and since I was an extremely analytical person naturally, the combination always worked in my favour.

This dream stuff was something different entirely. Not finding any answers in my reflection, just more questions, I walked back into my bedroom. Looking at the clock, I decided to call my best friend, Naomi, even though it was 10 minutes to midnight. I needed to talk to someone about this because I didn't want to go back to sleep. I took up my phone and hit the number two on the speed dial, praying she would pick up.

Naomi

The sound of Prince's *Baby I'm a Star* mingled with the image of me at six years old sitting on a playground talking to a purple giraffe.

"Naomi, are you going to answer the phone?" the giraffe asked.

"What?" I looked at the giraffe puzzled. "I thought we were going to take a walk to the park?" I replied, confused.

"We can still walk to the park, but are you going to answer your phone? Gina is calling," the giraffe announced.

Looking down at my hand, the glow of my iPhone and its rapid vibrating as Prince sang loudly brought me out of the depths of sleep. Finally focusing my eyes, I hit the accept button. "Hello?" I croaked.

"Hey, I know it's late, but I need to talk to you!" Gina said in a frantic high-pitched voice.

I looked at my clock which read 11:53 PM and laid back on my pillow with a puff. I'd only been asleep for 20 minutes after being at the hospital for a sixteen-hour shift.

"G, this had better be an emergency because if it's not, I promise I'm going to kill you! You know I have to be at the hospital in a few hours!" I was in my last rotation of emergency medicine in residence at the largest trauma centre in the city. I loved it, but the residency was brutal.

"Naomi, you know I would never call you at this time of night without it being something important. Have you heard about Veronica Bridges?" she blurted out.

"Veronica Bridges? G, what the hell are you talking about?" I asked, completely annoyed.

"She's a social media personality who went missing a few days ago, and I've been dreaming about her," she finished, almost whispering.

"Hmm, did you take an Ambien, drink some wine, and watch some of your True Crime shows again before going to bed? I'm going back to bed! I'll call you on my break to check on you," I said, getting ready to hang up the phone.

"Naomi, I have been dreaming about a real girl that is really missing and if I don't do something, she's going to die! I know this sounds crazy, but I don't know who else to talk to! This is crazy to me too; that's why I'm calling you. Please help me!" she pleaded.

I had never heard Gina plead for anything. That immediately shook the last bits of sleep from my mind. I reached over and turned on the lamp on the nightstand.

"Okay, Gina, what is going on? What are you talking about? You are dreaming about a missing girl? Start from the beginning," I said, sitting up in my bed. I knew I wasn't going back to bed any time soon.

When she finished recounting the initial dream, seeing Veronica on the news, and her recent dream where she was being raped and tortured, I was speechless with disbelief.

"Maybe the second dream is just a result of you seeing her on the news and your very active imagination," I offered.

"Then how do you explain the first dream? Naomi, I know it sounds crazy! I know it sounds straitjacket, padded walls, insane asylum crazy, but you know me! I would never call you if I didn't believe that what's happening is really happening!" Gina almost screamed. I had to move the phone away from my ear.

Pausing for a moment to allow her words to settle on my understanding, I considered again everything she had told me. "Do you think it's some kind of psychic thing?" I asked. Gina was the strangest person I knew. She always knew when my mom or sisters were calling without seeing the caller ID. She told me that my college boyfriend would cheat on me within five minutes of meeting him, and she was right. She knew I was accepted in the grad program just by picking up the envelope. She just knew things instinctively.

"I thought about that, even though I'm not exactly sure how that could be. But whatever the case, I have to do something!" she said desperately.

"Maybe you should call the cops?" I suggested.

"And tell them what? I had two dreams about the missing girl. No, Officer, I don't know who took her or where she is, but I just know that the bastard is going to rape her repeatedly before he kills her. They'll think I'm a fucking psycho or an accomplice to the fucking psycho that has her," Gina ranted.

"Hey, calm down! I'm not the enemy. I was just trying to help! Maybe you'll have another dream, and now that you are *aware*," I said emphasizing the word aware, "maybe you will be able to remember something you can take back to the police. Maybe I can hypnotize you and you do your psychic connection thing and we find out where Veronica is."

"Hypnotize me? Come on, Naomi. I'm trying to find a real solution here!" she said annoyed.

"You know I can do it. Don't you remember? It's how I paid my way through junior year of college working for that sideshow. If this truly is some sort of psychic thing, it's happening while your subconscious mind is in control. That's probably why it's happening when you're asleep. If you really want to help this girl, it can't hurt to try," I shrugged, forgetting she couldn't see me.

"Okay, maybe you're right. It can't hurt to try. Can you meet me at my place tonight after your shift at the hospital?"

"I'll be right there after I stop back home to feed Sparky," I said, and Gina clicked off the line.

Rubbing my face slowly with my hands, I thought, *What the FUCK just happened?*

Gina

D riving to work, all I could think about was Veronica and tonight's impending session of hypnosis with Naomi. My mind battled itself about whether something like this would really work. Rationally, I was very sceptical, but I was also determined to try to do anything to help this girl. I had almost been the victim of a date rape in college, and ever since, I had a desire to protect those who couldn't protect themselves. It's why I stayed in shape, trained hard to have a brown belt in Karate, and chose to work in private securities. The information I acquired and relayed to the field teams rescues real people from real-life monsters. Even though I was not hands-on with the monsters, what I did was vital. I located them. I had to look at this thing with Veronica no differently. I had to find the monster that had her and send the Calvary in to do the rest.

Derek

The dank atmosphere of the old pottery factory was dimly lit. It smelled of mildew and rotten clay. It was one of the reasons he bought the place. It was his "Man Cave," even though the size and configurations of it was closer to a lab than the typical space designated solely for male occupation. Derek had taken his time renovating the old space to ensure that it provided everything he would need to play. He had maintained part of the original design, in case anyone ever decided to take a look at the old factory. Furnished with an old kiln, other pottery tools and a mirrored wall, it doubled as his workout space. Something about the primitiveness of the exposed beams and dirt floors spoke to his animal side, and since this area was where his inner animal could run free, it seemed fitting. As he did military-style push-ups on the dirt floor, he took in, with long deep breaths, the unique smell it omitted. Most people would find the musty smell of spoiled earth unpleasant, but he liked it. It reminded him of the beginning smells of decomposition.

He completed his last push-up, rose, and flexed his arm and chest muscles. Watching the reflection of his muscles rippling in the mirror he stood in front of, his eyes settled on the long jagged scar that ran down his left flank from his armpit to the front of his groin, a forever souvenir from a bully many years ago. He thought about how mercilessly he had been ridiculed as a child, born with several health problems including a cleft pallet, which effected his appearance, and hyperthyroidism, which delayed his growth. The torment had been nonstop. He worked out obsessively once he finally had a growth spurt. He wasn't the short, ugly kid that was the victim of peer violence daily anymore. Now, he was six-feet-five-inches, muscular, wiry, and, thanks to plastic surgery, handsome. He was powerful and no one could ever take that away from him again.

His body pulsed with adrenaline from the workout and the memories. It made him feel animalistic—primed him for his play. He liked to work out before playtime to get his body ready for both the mental and physical requirements to do what he most enjoyed. Ready to get the night started, he went to the left side of the mirror and double-tapped the upper corner. A hidden door opened silently, revealing the stairway to his favourite part of his cave. Making it to the bottom of the stairs, he walked anxiously down the earth covered tunnel; he could barely contain the excitement that coursed through him. Arriving at a large steel door, he punched in numbers on an electronic keypad. The door opened and his adrenaline surged again.

Walking into the heart of his "Man Cave," he marvelled at Veronica who was laid in a horizontal flayed position strapped to the custom-made steel table, unconscious from the drugs he'd given her after their last playtime. His eyes lit up at the sight of the bruises and cuts that covered her body. She passed out several times during their play, and each time, he woke her with more pain. He really enjoyed seeing how women responded to pain. He'd been a little rough with Carrie once when he was first starting out. She was so weak that she cried just because he bit her. She didn't let him touch her for a month after that.

Walking over to Veronica's still body, he inspected the cuts for infection and found none. As much as he wanted to hurt her, he needed her to last until he decided otherwise. He'd cleaned and stitched up her wounds before giving her meds, just to show her that he did care about her health. Before he was kicked out of medical school, he had acquired the knowledge he needed to keep his playmates "healthy" until he was done with them. He was an expert in anatomy even before medical school. It was a part of his obsession with how things worked. Tonight would be even more fun; he planned to introduce her to some of his homemade toys. Building was one of the few things he learned from his father, and it was a lot safer to make his own toys than buy them. They were almost untraceable.

He decided to wake her with an especially painful creation, his version of a Gansu knife like the Japanese chefs use. Its sharpness and design allowed for him to easily slice the skin off in layers. He'd attached an electrical component to the handle that connected to the blade, and when activated, it cauterized the area as he sliced. It was really efficient because it minimized bleeding and allowed him to take his time with the parts he liked. Locating a strawberry-shaped bruise on her left shoulder, he started to slice away her skin.

Veronica

I screeched as hot blazing pain vibrated through my shoulder, ripping me from unconsciousness. The pain was disorienting. I felt his finger trace the place where the pain throbbed, and I screamed again. The stinging burn felt like he'd dipped his fingers in lemon juice.

"Veronica, my dear, you're awake," he said casually as if he hadn't just sliced a piece of my flesh off. "I have something very special planned for you. It's going to be even more fun than last time," he said jubilantly as he traced the left side of my collarbone with the tip of his blade.

I was not blindfolded anymore, and for the first time, I could see parts of him. He was shirtless, muscular, and from the angle at which he stood, I could see a long, jagged scar that ran from under his left arm to the front of his stomach and disappeared into the waist of his pants. I wondered if he had gotten it from a girl like me, one of his victims. I could tell he was tall, but the angle my head was in didn't allow me to move to see his face clearly. I tried to remember as much as I could about him, just in case I got out somehow; maybe I could identify him. As he moved to a table nearby, I noticed he had a slight limp, and there was a dip indentation on the right side of his back.

He turned and the puffy scar seemed to be dancing as his ribcage expanded rapidly. "Has any of those rich boys you like to fuck ever shown you the real meaning of carnal knowledge?" he said as he started to undo my bindings. As the ropes were loosened, the sensation of pins and needles exploded throughout my body, and I fell to the floor. His strong hands picked me up with the ease of a parent picking up their toddler. He placed me faced down on the steel table. Before I could begin to imagine what would happen next, he entered me anally. I felt my flesh rip.

29

Gina

"Eight, nine, ten... Open your eyes... G, come back to my voice. Gina, open your eyes...come back to the sound of my voice."

The sound of Naomi's calm voice ripped me away from the pain that permeated through my body. I blinked my eyes rapidly. My breath was caught in my chest along with the pain of the vision still coursing through me and I struggled to get my bearings. I felt like I was spinning as if I was caught between the pain and the sound of Naomi's voice. Opening my eyes widely, I focused on Naomi's round cocoa toned face—I'd always thought she looked like a Brazilian fairy—her hazel-green eyes stared intensely back at me, waiting.

"G, are you with me?" Naomi asked, concerned.

"Yes," I whispered.

"Did you make the connection?"

Flashbacks of the things he did to her bombarded my mind. "Yes, I did," I answered quietly.

"What did you see?" she asked, gently sitting on the edge of her chair.

"He...he sliced her skin, he played with her flesh, and I could feel everything. It stung like lemon juice...he, he sodomized her Naomi!" I said with fear and disgust thick in my words. Tears began to silently stream down my face.

"Calm down, G... Breathe." She scooted closer to the edge of her chair. "Did you see his face?"

"No, but I did see other things," I offered.

"Did you see anything that could help us identify him or where he is?" she probed harder.

The images of the vision rapidly replayed in my mind. To get the information I needed, I forced myself not to focus on the torture, but only him. "He's white, but his skin is tanned and he's tall... I tried to see, but I couldn't see his face because he is so tall!" I said with a bit of shock as the facts registered. "He has a long scar on his left side; it's ugly, all puffy and jagged," I paused to recall what Veronica remembered, what I remembered. "He has a limp and a deep dimple or indentation or something in his back," I blurted out. Tears ran down my face as I could no longer stop all the memories from overwhelming me. I felt my body cringe as my mind saw again the horrors he had inflicted.

"Gina, come back. Take some deep breaths for me," Naomi said, kneeling in front of me.

I did as she asked, taking three deep breaths, and my body slowly let go of some of its rigidness.

"Can you remember where you were, G? Anything unique about the space?" Naomi inquired.

"It smelled funky, like mildew and earth." I tried to remember the space he was working out in. "There was pottery; like maybe it was an old studio or something," I answered.

"Okay, so we have a tall white male. How old would you guess he is?" she asked.

I thought about it. "From the tightness of his skin, I don't think he's that old. Maybe early thirties," I guessed.

"Okay, so we have a tall, white, thirty-something-year-old male with a significant scar on his left side. He has a limp and some kind of strange dimple on his back. Do you remember what side?"

Thinking hard, I answered, "Umm... I believe it's his right side."

"Okay, I think we have something, G. We have the beginnings of a physical description and possibly a location," Naomi said with excitement in her voice.

"Naomi, I don't know if that's enough! I have to stop him. The way he's torturing her, she's not going to last much longer!" I said between sobs.

"G, take a few more deep breaths. You have to calm down! I know you want to help her, and we can use this information to go to the police," she encouraged, rubbing my arm comfortingly.

"They're going to think I'm crazy, or trying to get my 15 minutes of fame," I said solemnly.

"What if you talk to the retired military guy at your job? You're always talking about how he's the best investigator at the firm," she pointed out.

"You're right. I guess, I could talk to Neil. He is the best, and I know he respects me. He's told me on more than one occasion that I would have been a top-notch soldier."

"That sounds like your best option, especially if you don't want to go to the police."

"Think I should call him?"

"I think if you want him to take you seriously, it should be a face to face conversation."

"Yeah, you're right. I'll call him to see if we can meet somewhere," I said while taking my phone out of my pocket. I touched a few buttons to access our company's directory, found Neil Stamp's company cell number, and punched it in. I took a deep breath as it began to ring.

Neil

Miss Katie's diner was a hot spot for college kids and creatives. With its 50s style décor, classic All-America menu, and cheap prices, it was always packed. I pulled into the cramped parking lot and immediately felt uneasy by the number of people I could see from the large front windows. I had no idea what Porter needed to talk to me about at a place like this, but I knew her well enough to know she would have never asked me to come if it wasn't important. I touched the butt of the Sig Sauer that I had in a holster in the small of my back and readjusted the .22 I had concealed under my right pant leg. As an Army CID Warrant Officer, I was required to carry my weapon everywhere I went. Since retiring due to a shootout with an AWOL soldier I'd tracked down for raping several company members that left me hospitalized for months, I never went anywhere unarmed.

Opening the door to the diner, I spotted Porter immediately in a corner booth in the back of the room. Snaking my way back to the booth, my mind went through all the possible scenarios that Porter could be in to request to meet after hours. As she spotted me , she got up and moved to the other side of the booth. She'd worked with me long enough to know that I never sit anywhere with my back towards people. I surveyed the room before settling my eyes on her then slid into the room. I instantly noticed the dark circles under her eyes, the tightness of her face, and her dishevelled ponytail. I knew whatever she wanted to speak to me about was serious and weighing heavily on her because I'd never seen her appearance look anything less than perfect.

"Thank you for meeting me tonight, Neil," she began speaking in a low tone.

"Porter, what's going on?" I asked, wasting no time on small talk. I was a naturally forward person, but my time in the military had enhanced that characteristic tenfold.

"Let me start by saying that I know what I am about to tell you is going to sound unbelievable, but please hear me out. Have you heard about the missing girl, Veronica Bridges?"

"Yes, I read about her in the paper a few days ago, but I hadn't heard anything about the firm being involved in the case?" I said, puzzled.

"It's not a firm case, but I have information about it that I need your help with."

"If it's not a firm case, then how do you think I am supposed to help? If you have information, just go to the cops," I said a bit irked.

"Neil, I've been dreaming about Veronica. I dreamed about her kidnapping before I even heard about her being taken. I have had two more dreams that have shown me that she's being raped and tortured, and the freak that has her is going to kill her soon. The dreams have provided me with a little bit of info, but I don't think it's enough to go to the police with. I have to do something to stop this guy. You are the best tracker I have ever seen in my career and so, I think you can help me find her." She said everything in a rush, her voice so low I even struggled to hear her.

"Porter, you're not making any sense. What do you mean you have been dreaming about this missing girl and you want me to help you find her?" I asked, leaning forward.

She ran her hand through her hair, looked around the diner, then answered, "I know it sounds crazy. I can't really explain it. I have some kind of psychic connection that has allowed me to 'see' what is happening with Veronica and her kidnapper."

"If you want me to believe this, you are going to have to start at the beginning, because right now, I am trying my best to not get up and walk out on you," I said bluntly.

She took several deep breaths before she looked directly into my eyes and began talking. I took out a small notebook and began jotting down things as I allowed her to tell the story completely without interruptions, before asking her to start again. As she retold the story, I stopped her at different points to inquire about things I'd written down the first time. I asked her to tell the story for a third time to ensure that I'd heard everything correctly, and to make sure I'd asked all the questions I'd thought of. Feeling that I'd gotten all the information she could provide me, I sat quietly, going over my notes.

"Neil, can you please say something?" she asked, her voice heavy with insecurity.

"Porter...I've seen and done a lot in my life, but this is way out of my realm of understanding. I don't believe in psychics."

"You have said many times yourself that you don't know how I just 'know' how to find the guys we go after. I know you don't believe in psychics, but I need you to believe that what I have dreamt is happening! I have to do something, and I figured with all of the knowledge and skills you have..." she stopped speaking as my cell phone began ringing in the inner pocket of my jacket.

"It's your friend Mark. He's back from vacation," she said matter-of-factly as I took the phone from the inside of my coat.

My eyes widened slightly as I saw the name on the caller ID. "Mark, can I give you a call back later? I'm in the middle of something," I said rapidly.

"It's cool, I just wanted you to know I was back from vacation. Jenny and I are about to go get dinner, just call me when you get a minute," Mark said to me happily.

I hung up the phone, put it back in my pocket, and looked at her. "How did you know that was Mark calling? I've never mentioned his name to you before. How did you know?" I asked more to myself than to her directly.

"I don't know how to explain it, Neil. I just do. It's a feeling. It's always just been a feeling until now."

I sat back and covered my face with my large, scarred hands, blowing my breath out slowly. I again looked her in her eyes, "Listen, if we are going to do this, we have to make a plan. I've never gone into a mission blind, and as freaky as this shit is, I don't plan to start now. I have a few connections in the police department. I'm going to run this past them."

"Do you really think they'll listen?"

35

"I served with these guys, so they know me."

Carrie

I heard the beep of the alarm on the downstairs doors go off. I looked at the clock. It read 2:30 AM. Derek hadn't been home in two days and the litany of curse words that I'd rehearsed in my head this whole time were eager to be said. I didn't immediately get up from the bed because I wanted to see what he would do. The last time he did this, he didn't even try to explain himself. He just completely ignored me. Well, he wasn't going to do that this time! This time, I was going to tell him exactly how I felt. I was sick and tired of him always being gone, and never helping me with our children. He never did what I asked him to do around the house and to make things worse, I received a notice from the water company that the bill hadn't been paid in three months!

Maybe he's cheating on me, and if he is, I am leaving this time. I can't take this anymore. I should have listened when everyone told me not to marry him! I thought they were wrong. I thought I knew him better than anyone else and could change him! He has become stranger and colder over the years.

The sound of the bedroom door opening halted my mental rant. He entered the room and went to our master bathroom without even looking my way. As the sound of the shower coming on registered in my ears, I could no longer resist my need to confront him. The anger that coursed through my body caused the baby to kick me viciously in the ribs, adding to my fury. Getting out of the bed, I waddled quickly to the bathroom door. Throwing the door open, I simultaneously began to cuss.

"Where the fuck have you been, Derek? It's been two days! Are you fucking someone else?"

"Carrie, go back to bed. I want to take a shower," he said flatly, folding the shirt he'd taken off.

"I'm not doing anything until you tell me where you've been for the last two days!" I yelled, unable to control myself.

"You're going to wake the kids. Stop yelling. I needed a breather. Work has been really stressful."

"Stressful. You have no fucking idea what stressful is! I never get to take a breather because I am the only one taking care of our *five* kids. Not to mention that I'm eight months pregnant!" I yelled over the continued sound of the shower.

"You are the one who decided to be a fucking breeder, Carrie! Leave me the fuck alone so I can take a shower in peace!" he roared back at me, slamming the shower knob off.

I pushed him in the shoulder. "A breeder? Did you just call me a fucking breeder?" I screamed. "How fucking dare you! Did I fuck myself, Derek? You don't get to fucking check out this time! I am not going to take this shit anymore!"

His hand was around my throat before I could get another word out. The tightness of his fingers was like a vice. He put his face close enough to me that I could feel his minty breath that was now coming in short pants. The deadly look in his cold grey eyes sent a chill through my body.

"I told you to leave me the fuck alone," he said through clenched teeth, tightening his grip. I clawed at his hand as my chest burned from the lack of oxygen. He began to bang my head against the wall, as his grip became tighter still.

"You fucking sorry nag! I should kill you right now!"

He banged my head again hard enough to make me see stars. The lack of oxygen and the pure disbelief of what was happening prevented me from reacting to this statement. I could feel myself begin to lose consciousness as my baby kick wildly inside of me. Just when I thought I could no longer hold on, he let me go. I slid to the tiled floor like a puppet cut from strings. I coughed instinctually as I gasped to fill my lungs with air.

He grabbed my hair and dragged me into the bedroom. I tried to scream for him to stop but a strange raspy gargle was all that came out. He threw me on the bed and slapped me hard across my face. My lip split.

"I just wanted to come home to take a shower," he roared, slapping me again. I began to choke on my own blood and spit. "You just don't know how to shut the fuck up!" He punched me in my jaw, and I heard a loud crunch reverberate in my skull. "You're such a fucking cunt!" he said, wrapping his hands around my throat again. I could hear one of the kids knocking at the door, calling for me. I tried to fight him off, but the weight of his body was too much. I tried to kick at him, but the size of my pregnant belly prevented me from lifting my legs to get the angle to hit him. Unable to fight him any longer, all I could think of was the child moving wildly in my stomach, and I passed out.

***

The repeated sound of the doorbell, as well as the sound of children crying, brought me out of the darkness. The dizziness that covered me hit me with a wave of nausea that caused me to choke. I looked around for Derek as I struggled to get up but didn't see him anywhere. The doorbell rang again followed by a loud knock, and a voice announcing that it was the police. I stumbled to the door, trying to get my bearings as I went. Opening the door, a male and female officer stood looking back at me.

"Ma'am we were called here due to a report of a domestic situation. Do you need an ambulance?" the female officer asked.

"...I...I don't know what you're talking about," I managed to croak out.

"Ma'am, you're bleeding. Can we please come in? Who did this to you?" the male officer asked rapidly.

Before I could say another word, my oldest son, Thaddeus, answered, "Daddy did it! He's gone now, but he did it."

The female officer called for an ambulance with the radio from her belt, as the male officer helped me over to the couch. My mind whirled as I caught a glimpse of my swollen, bruised and bloody face in the mirror over the fireplace. *He really tried to KILL ME!*

"Ma'am, what's your name?" the female officer asked, kneeling in front of me.

"Carrie," I answered in a whisper.

"Carrie, tell me what happened."

The beating flashed through my mind, and the fear of Derek radiated through my body; I was speechless. Tears began to fall from my eyes. I had tried to keep things together for so long. I tried to handle his coldness, pretending it was just that he was socially awkward, but deep down, I knew it was more. He used to give me so much attention. Now, all he did was look at me with disgust. He didn't even try to interact with the kids anymore. He was always gone, and here I was still worried about him. I was not going to save him anymore. He tried to kill me!

I slowly told the officers what Derek had done to me between sobs. The story that fell from my swollen bloody lips didn't feel like it had just happened to me, but the pain I felt in every part of my body confirmed it had. The EMTs arrived just as the officers asked if I had any idea where Derek might be.

"He may be at work. Burk's Industries. It's a research laboratory in Brookfield. The only other place that he might be is at the pottery factory out past Ryan road." As I said this, I felt an acute pain rip across my lower abdomen, then my water broke and I screamed.

"Excuse us, officers, we have to transport her right now! The baby's coming!" one of the EMTs said.

"Thaddeus, take your siblings next door to the Honey's and tell them I'm having the baby!" I managed to get out as the EMTs hurriedly wheeled me out of the door.

Neil

The sound of the rain on the window of my study was the only thing keeping my nerves in a state of calm. I hadn't felt this uneasy since my time in the Army, before dangerous missions. I replayed the conversation with Porter, and the decision to actually tell someone else about the revelation of her dreaming of the missing Veronica Bridges. I knew for sure I was losing my mind. I had spent the last hour trying to find the words to say to my old military buddy, Vince, and still hadn't come up with anything. I tried to focus on the most important part of Porter's story—a girl was being raped and tortured—and if Porter was right, she would be murdered soon. Settling on this grim outcome, I knew I had to make the call.

My hands felt heavy as I punched in Vince's number and activated the call. Listening to the phone ring, I almost hung it up, but Vince answered before I could.

"What's going on, Stamps?" Vince greeted me happily in his raspy baritone voice.

"Vince, I need to talk to you. What's your location?"

"I'm at the station. What's wrong?" Vince asked with all the happiness drained from his voice.

"I have a very time-sensitive situation I need to discuss with you as soon as possible. Is it possible for me to come down there? I can be there in twenty."

"Ah...okay. You can come down, but can you give me some idea of what the hell this time-sensitive situation is about?"

"It's too sensitive for the phone. I'll see you in exactly 20 minutes." I hung up. I stood, checked my weapons, grabbed my jacket and rushed out of the door.

Darting through traffic faster than I should have for the rainy condition, I tried to figure the best way to breakdown what I needed to say to Vince without him laughing in my face. It was such a hard story to believe, but after hearing Porter's pleas, I knew I had to do something.

When I arrived at the station, I parked in the visitor's lot and ran inside to prevent being soaked by the sheets of falling rain.

The station was bustling with activity, as uniformed officers and civilians occupied several areas in the front lobby. Walking up to the information desk, I eyed a group of kids. One was trying to stick his hand up a vending machine unsuccessfully. A small-framed, mouse-faced man with a cowlick and thick-rimmed glass sat behind the desk. He didn't look old enough to drive a car, but his police uniform and gun belt said otherwise. I looked at the name tag on the left side of his baggy uniform shirt, "Smith, I'm here to see Sergeant Hightower. I'm Neil Stamps. He's expecting me."

Smith pushed his thick glasses up and picked up the receiver of the phone next to him and made a call. A few moments later, he hung up the phone, handed me a visitor's pass, and told me to take the elevators to the third floor.

Vince was waiting for me at the doors of the elevator when it arrived. He took me into a small conference room off the left side of the department floor. Cracking the door, he motioned for me to take one of the first two seats on the left side of the square table. He looked at me with intensely curious dark eyes. His puzzlement was written clearly on his face.

"Okay, spit it out, Stamps. What is this time-sensitive situation you need to talk to me about?"

Taking a moment before answering him, I said a small prayer asking that I use the right words to get him to listen to me.

"Vince, we've known each other for a long time. You know what kind of person I am. We've fought and almost died together, so you have to think about that when I tell you what I am about to tell you," I began.

"Stamps, what the fuck is going on? You're scaring me, man."

"Vince, just listen," I said, and retold the story that Porter had told to me down to the details of the physical description and the possible location of the pottery factory.

Sitting slowly back in his chair, Vince didn't say anything for a very long time.

"So, you want me to believe that one of your co-workers is dreaming about the missing girl, Veronica Bridges, being raped and tortured by a psycho tall white guy with a limp in some old pottery place?" Vince asked, hiding none of his disbelief.

"He has a bad scar and a deep indention on his back," I added.

"Whatever the fuck, Neil. What am I supposed to do with that?" Vince said almost yelling.

"Vince, I know," I began anew, but was interrupted when a petite dark haired Hispanic uniformed female knocked on the door.

"Sergeant Hightower, I just got the call from Lopez and Williams," she started stepping in the room. "They were finally able to get some information from the wife in that domestic call from this morning. They said that the husband owns an old pottery factory out in Pleasantville, and they were going to head out there, unless you have other orders."

At the mention of the pottery factory, Vince and I looked at each other with surprise.

"Did you say a pottery factory?" Vince asked anxiously.

"Yes, Sir."

"Do they have a description of the husband?" Vince asked hurriedly.

"Yes, his name is Derek Sparrow. He's 6'5", White, 165 lbs., and apparently, he walks with a limp."

My mind exploded as her words registered. Vince's mouth hung open. She looked at us both with a bit of confusion.

"Sir? What should I tell them?" she asked a bit impatient.

Closing his mouth and regaining his composure, Vince instructed, "Have them go out to the location but tell them to just do surveillance on the area and report back immediately. Tell them to proceed with caution!"

After receiving his orders, she turned and was gone. Vince got up and closed the door before he said anything. "I don't know if this is your guy..." he started but I stopped him.

"Don't bullshit me, Vince. You heard what she said. She gave you basically the same description I gave you. This guy owns a fucking pottery factory. It's the guy!"

"We don't know if he's *the guy*. I will have my officers take a look and we'll see if anything looks suspicious," he responded with disbelief written all over his face.

"If this is the guy, I doubt if he's going to behave suspiciously while the cops are in his face."

"Stamps, I know. But if we go in there half-cocked, we could blow this, and the girl's as good as dead. Go home, let me look into this and I'll call you."

Derek

I paced back and forth on the dirt floor causing a small dust cloud between steps. *Fucking Bitch!* I said over and over in my mind as the images of the morning looped in my brain. I'd never lost control with Carrie before. I was furious with myself. The rag I still felt emitted from me like a nuclear reactor overheating. I could still feel her heartbeat pounding in my hands as I choked her. I had wanted to kill her, was eager to kill her, but the sounds of our children beating at the door crying for her had brought me out of my bloodlust. She had passed out by this time, and I just left her there on the floor as I'd quickly exited our home. I knew from the light on at the next-door neighbour's house at that hour meant they had heard the fight. I fucking hated my neighbours.

I knew I needed to get myself under control if I was going to deal with the possible repercussions of my earlier actions, but the animal inside of me demanded to be fed. I went to the mirror, double-tapped the left corner and ran down the stairs once the door opened. I sprinted down the tunnel to the large door and quickly punched in the numbers to open it. Stepping inside my favourite space, I felt my anxiousness turn to a much different kind of excitement as my eyes fell upon Veronica. Overcome with animalistic desire, I didn't even bother to remove my clothes or wake her as I climbed onto her body. Her eyes flew open as I brutally entered her, and savagely began pumping, trying to regain control of myself. The sounds of her shrieks echoed off the walls and inside of my head, causing me to pump even harder. I clawed at the stitches on her right breast, ripping the wound open, and laughing as she howled in pain. The sight of her blood mixed with her screams was intoxicating. I knew I would orgasm soon. The memories of Carrie's blood running down her face as I slapped her repeatedly added to my arousal, and I felt my seed explode from my body, releasing the anger that had threatened to make me come undone.

Veronica's body heaved heavily up and down as she sobbed uncontrollably.

"Don't cry, dear. That was just a warm-up. I needed to get a hold of myself, but I'm much better now," I said, stroking her hair gently. "I was thinking we could try waterboarding tonight. What do you think about that, darling?" I asked, delighted with the look of terror that filled her eyes at my words. "I can see how many times I can bring you to the verge of darkness and bring you back with the pain," I explained delightfully.

Just as I was about to say something else, I was interrupted by the sound of an alarm. I raced over to a set of monitors that were attached to the surveillance system I had wired to my property. On the screen, I saw a black and white police car, driving up the old gravel road to the factory. I cursed loudly.

I scrambled to clean myself off. Only checking my face, hands, and arms, I hurried up the stairs, cursing Carrie as I took them two at a time. Preoccupied by my ranting and the impending arrival of the cops, I didn't close the door on the mirror all the way. Looking out of the dirt-covered front factory windows, I saw the police car pull up and park in what was left of the old parking lot. I tried to quickly decide what to say to the police. I knew they were there because of Carrie, which meant I would probably go to jail. My heartbeat banged in my ears, as I internally tried to recall the laws on domestic violence. I couldn't go to jail. I had too many things to accomplish, and Veronica was downstairs. Peering out of the window, I could see that there were two cops inside of the car, but they weren't getting out. My anxiety increased tenfold. Instead of waiting for them to come to the door, I decided to go outside.

Lopez

Pulling up to the old factory, I saw a late model tan Camry parked in a space next to the front doors. Judging from the chipped paint, dirt-covered windows, and the overall rundown appearance of the place, I guessed it'd had been many years since the place had been in business.

"Well, it looks like the suspect is here; that's his car according to the vehicle description in the system," I advised.

"Do we know what this guy did exactly?" Williams questioned.

"He beat the shit out of his wife this morning, allegedly," I replied, putting up air quotes to emphasize the last word.

"So, why aren't we just arresting this guy?" Williams asked.

"Apparently, Hightower wants us to wait. Maybe he's trying to get a search warrant."

"Look, is that the guy?" Williams asked, motioning to the tall man who'd just stepped outside of the factory's front doors.

Williams quickly pulled up the suspect's info on the console, "Yes, that's him. What the hell do you think he is doing?"

"I don't know. Maybe he came out to scratch his balls," I offered sarcastically.

"Should we get out and approach him?"

"No, Hightower said nothing about engaging the guy."

"Look," Williams said, pointing at the suspect, "is that blood on his shirt?"

"I don't know if it is blood, but it definitely looks suspicious, especially since we know he was involved in a domestic this morning," I remarked.

"I think we should check him out up close."

"Hightower told us not to engage with him."

"Yeah, but he's not here to see a suspect with blood on his shirt," Williams said while opening his door.

"Williams, we're not supposed to engage him! Williams... SHIT!" I said as he exited the patrol car. I scrambled to catch up. We had been partners for five years now, but I had never gotten used to my partner's ability to bend the rules whenever he saw fit. Catching up to Williams, I quickly asked, "What are you going to say as to why we are here?"

"I can say we're canvassing the area. He doesn't need to know exactly why," Williams replied curtly.

"Hightower is gonna have our asses if this goes wrong in any way!" I said in a low tone as we approached the suspect.

"Can I help you, Officers?" Derek asked through clenched teeth.

"Yes, you can. I'm Officer Williams and this is my partner, Officer Lopez. Have you seen anything strange in the area?" Williams asked cheerfully, while resting his hand on the butt of his gun nonchalantly.

"Strange?" Derek asked curiously, as the muscles in his jaw flexed.

"We had a call that there were kids causing a disturbance in the area. Have you seen any kids joyriding around here? Maybe they caused some of the broken windows?" I asked, pointing to windows on the second floor.

"No, I haven't seen anything. There aren't many people around here, but if I see any kids, Officer Lopez, I will let you know," Derek said sarcastically.

"Do you mind if we take a look around the premises to see if there has been anything tampered with?" Williams asked in a tone that said he didn't really need permission.

"I said I haven't seen anyone," Derek said, shifting his weight from one foot to another, clearly annoyed.

"We're not trying to bother you, Mr.?" Williams paused questioningly to allow him to answer.

"Sparrow," Derek answered.

"Mr. Sparrow, we just want to ensure your safety, and stop some kids from getting themselves in a lot of trouble," Williams casually finished with a friendly smile.

"There's nothing here for kids to disturb; it's an old factory," Derek retorted matter-of-factly.

"Well, I'm sure you don't want your property destroyed, and we'd just like to be sure, Sir," I added, mirroring my partner's smile. Being partners with Williams for the last five years gave us the benefit of knowing each other's nonverbal cues. I knew that he was trying to get a better view of the inside of the factory, but Derek's wide frame blocked William's view.

Taking a step towards Derek, I said, "Mr. Sparrow, are there any areas on the property that you think would be a 'hot spot' for kids to disturb?"

Sparrow reacted the way I thought he would to my "invasion" of his personal space. He stepped back and turned into a defensive stance, which allowed Williams a much better view through the front doors.

"Look, I don't think there's any need for you to look around. I have something to do. Like I said, if I see something, I'll give you guys a call," Derek said with thick disdain, as he turned and walked back into the factory.

Looking at my partner, I smiled, "Well, I guess that's the end of that."

"I guess so, let's get back to the squad before Mr. Sparrow decides to lose his shit and come back out here. I would really hate to have to do the paperwork if something bad happened," Williams responded while walking back to the squad car.

"Did you see anything strange?" I asked as he walked around the front of the car to the driver's side door.

"I saw workout equipment and a large wall-length mirror, but it looked like there was a door on the left side of the mirror. I don't know about you, but that weirdo made the hairs on the back of my neck stand up. He's all kinds of bad! Pure evil! He has bad juju coming off him like a stench!" Williams announced while rubbing the back of his neck.

"Oh yeah, he's a fucking psycho, no questions about that! Hell, any guy that would beat on his eight-month pregnant wife and almost choke the life out of her is a piece of shit completely. Did you see how the veins were popping out of his head and neck while we were talking?"

"Stevie Wonder could've seen that! Do you think he's hopped up on dope?"

"I wouldn't put it past him," I said.

"So, what now?" Williams questioned.

"I am going to call Hightower to see how he wants us to proceed," I said as I hit the numbers on my phone.

Hightower picked up on the second ring, "What did you see, Lopez?"

"Well, we saw the suspect, Sir. We actually talked to him," I replied, bracing myself for the curse words I knew were coming.

"Talked to him? You were not supposed to engage with him!" Hightower said loudly.

"Sergeant Hightower, I know you said not to engage with the suspect but, he came right outside when he saw us pull up."

"What happened?" Hightower demanded loudly.

"We spoke to the suspect. He's a creepy son of a bitch, Sergeant. But we tried to get him to give permission for us to search the property," I started.

"Did he give permission?" Hightower asked impetuously.

"No, he was pretty clear that he didn't want us looking around."

"I'm working with Judge Haggerty now to get a search warrant," Hightower advised.

"Do you want us to arrest him on the domestic while you wait for the warrant?" I inquired.

"No. What is the surrounding area like? Any place that you can duck out of sight to watch this guy?" Hightower asked.

"We haven't had the chance to do a perimeter sweep yet, Sir," I admitted.

"What the fuck are you waiting for? Do the sweep and find a hole to hide in and watch until I call you back. If this dickhead makes a move, call me!" Hightower screamed and then hung up the phone.

Williams hesitated before asking what took place on the call, "How bad is it?"

"Long story short: he wasn't happy we engaged the suspect, and he wants a perimeter sweep along with a stakeout. If the suspect farts wrong, we're supposed to contact him immediately!" I reported.

"Why can't we arrest him for what he did to his wife?" Williams questioned.

I shrugged, "Look, I'm just the messenger and he told me that we are supposed to hunker down and watch."

"Where are we going to do that? Sparrow doesn't want us anywhere around here, I'm sure he's still watching—" Williams started.

I cut him off, "That doesn't matter, we have our orders and as much as I'd take a bullet for you, bro, I'm not taking one from Hightower!" I told him bluntly.

"Well, since you put it like that, I guess it's stakeout time."

Neil

It had been three hours since I'd left the station and Vince still hadn't called me back. I was looking at my watch for the seventh time in the last five minutes. *I'm making myself crazy*, I thought as I paced the shiny wooden floors of my den. After my conversation with Vince at the station, I sent a message over to Porter letting her know that I'd spoken to my source and had been doing laps in my office ever since. If I'd had a rug on the floor instead of wood, the hours' worth of walking would have been clearly evident in its pattern.

Unable to contain my curiosity, I decided to call Vince to find out what was going on. Dialling his number rapidly, I continued to pace as I listened to the phone ring.

"Hightower," he said, answering on the third ring.

"Vince, it's me, Stamps. Any updates?"

"Stamps, let me handle this," Hightower said with an annoyed tone.

"You wouldn't have anything to look into if I wouldn't have come to you with the information that I had. The least you can do is let me know if there are any updates," I said seriously.

Hightower let out a long breath before speaking again, "Neil, we are still investigating."

"Don't give me that political official investigation shit! Did you go out to the pottery factory or not? Did you find the guy?" I asked at a machine-gun pace.

"Yes, I sent a car out to the factory. You heard that when you were at the station. They did locate the suspect, but at this point, there's nothing I can do."

"What the fuck do you mean you can't do anything! You're the fucking police! I came to you to try to help this missing girl, but if you can't do anything, I obviously made a mistake," I said disdainfully.

"Neil, you know that I want to get this psycho as much as you do, but I have rules I have to follow to do so. I have a unit at the factory watching the place. So, if this guy makes a move, I'll know," Vince said calmly.

"He doesn't need to make a move, Vince. He has the girl there! You have to get inside that place before he kills her!"

There was a long pause before Vince spoke again, "Look, Neil, I'm going to check something and call you back," and he clicked off.

The long string of cuss words that spewed from my lips would have made my mother slap me across the room. I knew that the police took their own sweet time when investigating, but I didn't think I'd get that from my own friend. *I have to get her out myself*, I thought as I sat down for the first time in hours.

Vince

Hanging up on Neil, I cussed loudly, "SON OF A BITCH!" As much as Neil had just pissed me off questioning me, he'd made me aware of something I overlooked when talking to Lopez. I'd been so pissed by them engaging Sparrow that I didn't get a chance to hear if they had actually seen anything suspicious. Dialling Lopez's number, I said a silent prayer, hoping he'd have something to tell me.

"Yes, Sir," Lopez said answering the line on the second ring.

"While you engaged the suspect, did you or Williams see anything funny?"

"We think the suspect had blood on his shirt, and Williams saw a mirror door inside, but couldn't really see anything else," Lopez quickly reported.

"Blood on his shirt? Are you sure?" I asked impatiently.

"Yes, Sir. It looked like blood. Not a significant amount, but blood, nonetheless," Lopez said.

"Did you take a look around the place?" I inquired.

"We did, Sir. This place is a lot bigger than it looks from the road. There are three other entrances besides the front doors, but they all had chains and padlocks on them. All the back windows on the first floor are boarded up, except for the ones in the front of the building. The fire escape from the second floor has been removed. We didn't get the chance to look around the west side of the building because there isn't a road that way and you asked us to stay out of sight," Lopez finished.

"Have you seen Sparrow since you spoke to him?"

"No, Sir."

"Okay, is there any chance he left without you seeing?"

"No, I don't think so, Sir. We tried to keep eyes on the areas of the factory that we have access to the whole time," Lopez answered nervously.

"Keep your position. Let me know if anything, and I mean if ANYTHING, changes."

Gina

I looked at my phone knowing the call was coming before it rang. Neil was calling. I answered on the first ring. My gut started to do flips as his first words touched my ears.

"Porter, I made contact with my friend that's a cop," he began with a grave tone.

"And he's not doing anything with the information you gave him about Veronica," I finished flatly.

"Yes. How did you know that?" he asked with an uneasy sound in his voice.

"Neil, we've been over that part already. Spidey senses in my gut, remember? Of course, you do. Now, moving right along. What are you planning?" I asked, cutting out all of his small talk. I knew what he was going to say before he said it, but I needed him to say it anyway. It was more for him than me.

He was silent for a few moments before he spoke again. "I'm going to that factory. Vince is talking about a warrant but fuck a warrant! Veronica's life is on the line!" he said passionately.

"I'm going," I said stoically.

"What? Wait...no you're not! I will not put you in that kind of danger, Porter!" Neil said slamming his hand down hard on something to emphasize his point.

"Neil, I'm a big girl! You know I can handle this. Besides, you need me," I said evenly.

"Porter, you are not going!" he strongly insisted.

"How are you going to get in?" I questioned acerbically.

"I'm going to recon the place and find the best point of entry."

"That's a great concept and all Mr. Army guy, but he'll know you're on the property before you even get close to a 'point of entry.'" I said the last part with much sarcasm in my voice.

"And how do you know that he will know that?" he questioned.

56

"Because he has a security system, and again, spidey senses," I reminded him.

"You never said anything about a security system," Neil said charged.

"I also haven't talked to you since the diner. He has the security system and a coded steel door that you have to access before getting to Veronica. I know you are the real-life G.I. Joe, but you need my help. Accept it. I'll come to your place and we'll make a plan and go save Veronica," I said flatly.

"Fine. Pick up a 12-pack of Millers on your way," he said and clicked off the line.

Derek

"This is all Carrie's fault. I should have killed her! Fucking BITCH!" I screamed as I paced frantically back and forth in front of the mirror. Punching at the air rapidly, I imagined each blow crushing a part of Carrie's body. "I should have killed her," I mumbled over and over. "Now everything is ruined. Now, I can't finish playing with Veronica all because of that fucking cunt wife! I should have fucking choked the life out of her!"

Grabbing fistfuls of my hair to try to get control, I knew I had to get out of here. My thoughts raced at light speed, and I struggled to catch hold of one. I shook my head trying to slow them down in between the string of curses that fell from my lips without my control. I felt my mind splitting as I punched the top of my head rapidly. Somewhere within the rage, the looping thoughts, and the voices, I had to get my shit together if I was going to make it out of here alive. I had to go to the escape plan. The thought made me stop pacing for the first time since I'd come back inside. Looking at my reflection, the sight of my own eyes helped me to regain a bit of control, but only the smallest bit. I knew I had to finish things here.

Veronica was unconscious on the table and as badly as I needed to touch her again to calm the beast inside of me, I knew I couldn't. I had to stick to the escape plan. Racing over to the security monitors, I could see the cop car from earlier parked behind a set of wildly overgrown hedges in a wooded area, about 300 yards away from the front of the factory. *Stupid cops think they can outsmart me,* I thought as I was glaring at the monitors. They had no idea of what I had in store for them, but soon enough, they would know my wrath.

Pulling my duffle off the shelf next to the monitors, I started to pack up my instruments. Each piece that I wrapped had a sentimental value. A memory of blood. A girl like Veronica was one of those privileged living Barbie dolls that were too spoiled and too entitled. I cut the vanity out of them, bit by bit, piece by piece, and enjoyed every second of it. It was my duty to punish as many of them as I could. They were all like her, that slutty whore that was my mother who opened her legs for any man that would show her a bit of attention and had money in his pocket, even her own brother, my father. She was the reason I was born with deformities and she was the reason why they all had to die.

Once I had my duffle packed with everything that could possibly identify me or any of my victims, I looked at Veronica for a very long time. Deep purple and black bruises covered her body like spots on a Dalmatian. The cuts across her breast and stomach made a swirling pattern across her skin. My arousal peaked and I struggled to stop my impulse to fuck her one last time. I broke my gaze and went over to the monitors to check on the cops. They hadn't moved from their hiding spot. I punch a few keys to make the camera zoom into their car. They were both asleep. Perfect.

Gina

I arrived at Neil's large two-storey brick home, with the 12-pack in hand and Naomi by my side, 45 minutes after our call. He opened the door before I could ring the bell.

"Porter, you didn't tell me you were bringing anyone with you," Neil barked.

I held the Millers up as a peace offering. "We need her," I said pushing past him.

"Hi. I'm Naomi," she said shyly in response to the stern look on Neil's face. He side-stepped to allow her to walk into the house.

He closed the door and we walked down the hall to the living room. "I didn't know you had this kind of taste, Neil," I remarked, looking around at the neatly arranged room. It was decorated in deep earth tones that accented the natural wood throughout the space. Several sculptures of various sizes and colours were smartly placed around the room as well as several paintings that hung on each wall. The focal point of the room was a brick fireplace that had the largest and most interesting painting above it. The painting was of a naked woman surrounded by planets in a vast universe; the constellations covered her most feminine parts. It was dynamic, with its vivid colours that seemed to move around the woman's body. "I love this painting. Who's the artist?" I questioned.

"Nubian Star. She's a personal friend of mine, but that's not important right now," he began, sitting down in a dark brown leather recliner. "Porter, we have to get this plan right if we are going to save her," Neil finished grimly.

"I know we do and that's exactly why I brought Naomi," I pointed my thumb towards her on the couch next to me. "I told you that I don't know how this psychic thing exactly works, but Naomi was able to help me tap into it with hypnosis. This ability—"

"Your superpower you mean," Naomi interrupted enthusiastically.

Smiling at my best friend, I went on, "Whatever it is, it's getting stronger, but I still can't call on it when I want. So, this is what I was thinking: she puts me under and you help her ask the questions we need to get the information that will help us. We make the plan. We execute the plan, save Veronica, and hopefully put a stop to this asshole once and for all. We save the day, the end," I finished wiggling my fingers theatrically, doing jazz hands.

Neil sat back in the recliner, signs of deep thought were all over his face, evident by the creased folds of his forehead. He seemed to be having a conversation with himself, and from the looks of it, it wasn't going well.

Naomi walked over to Neil and sat down next to him, "I know this is hard for you to accept. From what I heard, you're a pretty practical man. It was hard for me to accept too, but I have. And you have to as well. Gina has always told me how much of a brave and resourceful guy you are. Right now, you guys need to use every resource available to save Veronica," Naomi added, appealing to the soldier in Neil.

Neil took one of the beers from the 12-pack, opened it, and drank it down in one long gulp. "Let's get this hocus pocus stuff over with before I change my mind," he responded, grabbing another beer. "Let's go in the den; it's this way," he pointed to the left of the living room doorway.

He led us to a room at the very end of the hall which was covered in Army memorabilia. Looking around, there were several pictures of Neil in uniform, some formal, but most of them not. There was an American flag hung proudly on the wall in a shadowbox with several metals inside.

"Is that a Medal of Honor?" Naomi asked with astonishment on her face.

"Yes, it is," he replied, giving no other details.

"Wow. That's really impressive," Naomi stated.

"Thank you. But there's nothing impressive about killing people," he said with a stony tone, his eyes filled with pain. "What do we need to get started?" Neil inquired.

"First, G, you go in the other room while Neil and I decide what I am going to ask you. I think we will get a much better response without you knowing the questions ahead of time," she said to me. She turned to Neil, "Once we do that, then it's just a matter of getting Gina on the couch."

"Are you sure we shouldn't all discuss the questions to make sure you and I don't miss something?" he asked me.

"Neil, I think if we handle this the same way we do on the job, we'll get the information we need. I have faith in you. You'll know the right questions to ask," I said confidently. I got up and walked out of the room as Naomi instructed.

After 15 minutes of wandering around Neil's house admiring his very eclectic and masculine taste, Naomi found me in front of the Nubian Star painting again.

"You really like this painting," she said, startling me.

"I really do. I see Veronica. Well, honestly, I see us all in this piece," I answered, still looking at the painting.

"Are you ready, G?" Naomi asked gently.

"I'm as ready as I'm going to be."

"Let's do this," she said, putting her arm around my shoulder and squeezing me in a side hug.

Walking into the den, Neil was in a high-backed chair behind his giant mahogany desk that sat in front of the bay window. His face was still creased but this time it was determination I saw in his eyes. I knew at that moment he had his game face on.

"You ready, Neil?" I asked him seriously.

"As ready as I'm going to be," he answered, echoing the same words I'd spoken only moments earlier.

"Can we dim the lights in here?" Naomi asked.

Neil walked over to the wall switch and did as she asked.

I laid on the long leather couch that occupied most of the left wall of the den. Closing my eyes, I took a few deep breaths in, attempting to slow my heartbeat. When I started to feel a bit calmer, I opened my eyes. Naomi sat in a chair just outside my right peripheral view; I turned my head, nodding to let her know I was ready.

"Gina, close your eyes and take three deep breaths in for me. Breathe deeply into your nose, fill up your lungs with warm air, hold it... Now, breathe out of your mouth slowly. Feel the coolness of your breath cross your lips; push it all out. Good. Now, breathe in again. Feel your breath go all the way down to your toes. Hold it. One... Two... Three... Breathe out. Feel your body completely relaxing. Let go of the tension in your muscles," Naomi instructed in a quiet tone.

Naomi's voice was melodic and calming, relaxing me so much that I felt myself sinking into the soft leather of the couch. My heartbeat slowed as my breathing evened out. I felt myself letting go of everything except Naomi's voice. The familiar feeling of weightlessness blanketed my body. A tingling sensation ran from the base of my spine to the back of my skull. Images started to slowly come into focus like reels on an old home movie.

"What is he doing?" I heard Naomi ask, as I concentrated to make the dark frame come into focus. Closer and closer the frame came until it clicked into focus, and I know I had connected to him. I could see what he was seeing, feel the madness that was a part of every one of his cells. He was walking through a tunnel that emerged in a wooded area. Stepping outside, the eerie green glow from the night vision glasses he wore seemed to compliment the darkness that flowed through him. Keeping his steps light and silent, Derek made his way towards where he knew one of the cops was. The NV glasses allowed him to see Officer Lopez as he stood at a bush relieving himself, oblivious of Derek's presents. With the KA-Bar knife gripped tightly in his hand, Derek stepped behind Lopez, simultaneously placing his hand over Lopez's mouth as he pulled the blade slowly across the officer's throat. Derek couldn't see Lopez's face, but he could see him grabbing at the gushing wound on his neck. Derek relished what he envisioned was the shock that must have been plastered on the cop's face. He stepped back, letting Lopez's body fall silently to the dirt. He stood there for a moment, watching blood spill out of the man's body, exhilarated by the sight of it.

Slowly, Derek walked toward the spot occupied by the police cruiser and the other cop. Moving with almost inhuman speed, it took him less than a minute to make it to the opposite side of the hedge the cop car was parked next to. From his position, he could see Officer Williams sitting in the driver seat, his head back, eyes closed. The window of the cruiser was down, and the sound of Williams' snoring was amplified in the silence of the foliage. Derek crouched down as he left his hiding spot. He moved quickly to the side of the car. When he reached the window, he lunged inside with his knife, rapidly stabbing into Williams' throat. The sleeping man's eyes flew open, his hands flailed, and Derek continued stabbing him. Williams' blood sprayed the windshield and dashboard. Derek laughed a frighteningly sinister laugh as Williams weakly tried to grab at the hand holding the knife. In one final act of viciousness, Derek drove the KA-Bar through Williams' right palm and deep into his left eye socket. The cop jerked a few more times, then he was still.

Derek opened the police car door and pushed Williams over to the passenger seat. He climbed into the driver's seat and looked around. Finding a discarded fast food bag on the floor, he used it to wipe the windshield and started up the car. He drove the car to a thickly wooded area just outside of the property, by the old well, and parked there. He thought he would use the police car when it was time to leave. The cop car was not a part of his escape plan, but it was a welcomed bonus. Before getting out of the car, he grabbed the portable radio that was clipped to Williams' belt. He could use it to listen in to see if they were sending more cops. "And if they did send more, I'll cut Veronica's throat before they ever get here," he said to the night and laughed again as he walked back to the front entrance of the factory.

The sound of Naomi's gentle voice was misplaced against the deadly images that were playing in Derek's mind, it caught my attention immediately.

"... Completely disconnected from Derek once you hear me count to 10. One... Two... Three... Four... Five... Six... Seven... Eight... Nine...

Ten… Take a deep breath in, Gina. Good. Now, breathe out and open your eyes," she instructed.

Opening my eyes, it took me a few moments to settle back into my body. I still didn't like the feeling of activating my spidey senses with hypnosis. It was like waking up with a hangover, but 10 times worse.

"Take some more deep breaths. G, don't get up until you can fully feel your body again," Naomi directed. We'd done the hypnosis a couple of times since the first one, and I had told her all of the uncomfortable side-effects of the whole process, including the feelings of being disconnected from my body. I sat up slowly, looking first at Naomi, and then at Neil. He had moved from behind his desk and was now seated opposite of me in a sitting chair. His face was ashen.

"Did we get the info we needed?" I asked, sitting up slowly. It took a little bit for the memories of what I had seen to catch up to my conscious mind after the hypnosis.

Naomi looked down at the pad of paper in her lap filled with notes. "Yes, we did, and then some," she replied gravely.

"What?" I asked, looking questioningly at the both of them. "What did he do?" Even as the question came out of my mouth, the images of the memories started to become solid.

"He killed…" Neil began.

"Both of the cops," I finished as I could see exactly what he'd done flash before my mind. "He's revved up, almost completely out of control! If we don't get there soon, he's going to kill Veronica and disappear," I urgently warned.

"He can't get away. You're connected to him, right?" Neil asked, almost demanded.

"I don't know, Neil. I don't know if I'm connected to him or Veronica. I don't know why any of this shit is happening!" I yelled, losing control of myself. The mixture of Derek's craziness and my own emotions made my skin feel prickly and my brain felt like it was crawling with fire ants. I knew I was going to throw up. I jumped off the couch and just made it to the trashcan in time, as the contents of my earlier meal spewed from deep within me. In an instant, Naomi was at my side, holding my hair as I continued to retch. When I finally finished, I sat back on the hardwood floor and looked up at Neil's concerned face.

"I'm sorry, Gina. I didn't mean to push you," Neil offered gently. It was the first time he'd ever used my first name since I met him.

"What did you just call me? Don't you get soft on me now, Neil. We have a monster to catch."

My words seemed to smack away whatever bit of sentiment he was feeling. His normal steely glare came back into his eyes as he helped me up off the floor.

"Go clean up. Then let's get down to business," he said firmly.

An hour later, we'd worked out our plan to get Veronica out of the factory alive, and if all went the way Neil hoped, Derek wouldn't make it out at all. Thanks to Neil's military background and my own passion for guns, we had a small arsenal between us. Neil made a few calls and we were able to get ear coms and night vision glasses of our own. I had provided enough detail of the landscape and factory layout that Neil was able to draw up a pretty accurate rendition of the grounds to allow us to make a strategically executable rescue plan.

Neil and I double-checked each other's gear as well as made sure we had enough ammo to light up the night if needed.

"You guys look like you're extras in a mercenary movie, all decked out in your black paramilitary gear and guns. G, you never told me you were G.I. Jane in your spare time," Naomi joked, trying to lighten the mood.

"I told you I was a superhero in my secret life. Sometimes, I trade the leotard and cape for all-black paramilitary gear. I'm a versatile and fashionable superhero," I joked.

"Naomi, are you ready to do your part?" Neil asked, ignoring our amusing banter.

"I'm only driving you guys to the property line where I'll wait to call in your friend, Vince, with the Calvary. That's not exactly rocket science, Neil," Naomi retorted.

Giggling, I tried to reassure Neil. "Naomi likes to handle stress with humour," I explained. "Don't worry, she's tougher than she looks. Don't let the gentle demeanour fool you. This chick has snuck me out of more places than I care to admit," I stated.

"That's enough, G. Let's go!" Naomi said, grabbing me and pulling me towards the door.

We all climbed into Neil's black and chrome 2004 Hummer H3. Neil and I sat in the backseat of the mammoth truck while Naomi took the wheel. She looked almost juvenile behind the huge steering wheel. It was a good thing Neil's windows were tinted, or we might have been pulled over because someone could have mistaken Naomi for a teenage girl much too young to drive.

"Please buckle your seatbelts and keep your hands in your lap during the ride. Thank you very much for riding Rescue Mission Delta," Naomi said in a mock amusement park announcer tone as she pulled Neil's tricked out Hummer out of his garage.

During the ride, Neil sat quietly with a stoic look on his face. I could see that he was in deep thought. I apologetically interrupted him, "Do you want to look at the map and go over the entry plan one more time?" I asked. He didn't say anything as he pulled his copy of the map from his breast pocket.

He turned on a pin-sized flashlight and begun to speak. "Once Naomi drops us off on the other side of the property line, I will go through the secret well entrance on the south side of the property. You are going to go in on the west side, purposefully tripping the security alarms to get his attention. Assuming he responds to the tripped alarm and comes your way, once you tell me you have eyes on him, I'll come in and get Veronica." Now looking at Naomi, he added, "That's when I call you in. You zoom in and get Veronica out. After 15 minutes, make the call to Vince. I'll go find Porter. If she hasn't killed Sparrow, then God willing I'll get to snap this sick fuck's neck myself. Vince and the cop Calvary will arrive, and we will have saved the day. The end," he finished.

"Neil, can you explain to me again why you can't just have Vince and the cop Calvary meet us there? Why do you and my best friend have to do this?" Naomi questioned in a somewhat amused tone but also asking very seriously.

Meeting Naomi's gaze in the rear view mirror, Neil narrowed his eyes, "Your best friend and I," he started, "have to do this because, as we learned during the hocus pocus stuff, he has a police radio and if he hears the cops are on the way, Veronica dies. Vince is trying to handle this by the book by getting a warrant. If we wait on that warrant, Veronica dies. So basically, if we don't do this now, Veronica dies," he ended sternly.

"Oh yeah. I remember that now. I don't like it. I don't like it one tiny little bit, but we can't let Veronica die. Neil?" she said, looking back at him in the rear view mirror with deep concern in her eyes.

Returning her gaze, he replied, "Yes, Naomi."

"Promise you will bring my best friend back," she said, wiping away the tear that had escaped her eyelid. "Promise me!" she said louder and more seriously.

"I promise, Naomi. God willing," he replied.

"God willing it goes that smooth," I said in a whisper more to myself than to Neil. We rode the rest of the way in silence.

Veronica

H e stood above me, as he'd done so many times before since he'd taken me, but something in his eyes was different. He was sweating profusely and breathing heavily. He clenched his jaws so tightly together, I could hear his teeth grind.

"Veronica, my dear, I'm sorry to inform you that our time together has unfortunately come to an end. I know you must be sad of course, but you have to know this hurts me a million times more than you," he began, his voice rising and falling like some singsong sounding lullaby. "Because of that fucking cunt Carrie, I have to leave you," he said while he caressed my face. "I am not ready to leave you," he grabbed my mutilated left breast. "You've been one of my best catches, one of the best girls," he remarked sadly, dragging his fingers down the centre of my left forearm. "They are coming for you. Well, really, they are coming for me, but they will not catch me. And by the time they do get here, you'll be dead," he whispered as he slashed my forearm just above my wrist with a scalpel.

The feeling of pain didn't immediately register, but the warmth of my blood flowing down my arm as it began pooling in my hand did. He quickly cut my right wrist, and this time, the pain came quick and stinging as I realized this was the way I was going to die.

He drew in close to my right cheek. I could feel the hotness of his breath, smell the thick scent of mint as he spoke to me one last time, "Remember that I love…"

Before he could finish his words, an alarm sounded from the bank of keyboards and monitors. A terrifying look of rage crossed his face, and he bit down on my right cheek hard as he growled in anger. I felt the flesh from my cheek separate from my face as he pulled away and raced over to the monitors. I howled from the pain the radiated across my face and then I began to feel woozy, before I passed out.

Derek

I ran to the monitors and screamed in rage as I saw the woman creeping into a window on the west side of the factory. Slamming my hands against the keyboard, breaking it, I turned to kill whoever this woman was. Then I was going to leave this fucking place before I ended up in a jail cell. Storming down an access tunnel that would allow me to intercept this mystery woman, I felt something snap inside of me. My vision seemed to narrow, and the animalistic bloodlust consumed me. I was going to rip this woman's throat out with my bare hands.

I roared as I burst through the side door of the access tunnel, startling the woman, but she recovered quickly and launched a solid kick in my side. I hit the wall hard, but I didn't feel it. All I could feel was the need for blood racing through my veins. I bounced off the wall and went immediately to grab her. She took a defensive stand then delivered two quick jabs to the left side of my chest. The blows made me stutter step a little, but I continued forward, swinging hard at her face. My fist connected to the side of her head, and I heard her cry out in pain. I laughed loudly. She fell to her knees, recovering much quicker than I expected, and kicked out with her left leg. The blow landed in my abdomen, knocking some of the air out of me. She jumped to her feet and swung her knee in an upward motion, connecting it with my chin. I felt my bottom teeth slice through my tongue as my teeth crunched together. She quickly followed that up with an elbow to my face and I went down hard. She proceeded to kick me in my ribs and face until I reached out and grabbed her foot. She fell backward, and I jumped onto her, pressing all of my weight on her. I punched at her face, and she raised her hands in an attempt to block the severity of the blows. At the first sight of her blood, my adrenaline surged, and I rained down punches on her with all my strength. I saw her weakening as one of her hands fell away from her face. Then, suddenly, my entire body was on fire with electricity, my muscles went rigid, and I passed out.

Neil

Standing at the hidden door of the well entrance, I waited for Porter's signal. Even though I had been in combat situations before, it didn't stop my heart from beating loudly in my ears. I needed this mission to go right, and in truth, I needed to end this fucker before he hurt anyone else. I still felt uneasy about allowing Porter to be bait for Derek, but it made the most sense, especially if Veronica was as hurt as we thought. Porter wouldn't be able to carry her out if she couldn't walk on her own, I could, but that still didn't calm the uneasiness that flowed through me.

I heard Porter's voice in the ear com, giving me the signal to go. I rushed through the tunnel, swinging my Sig in up and down arcs. Counting off my steps, I knew that in a few more, I would be in what Porter called his lab. Making my way into the well-lit space, I took off the NV glasses and quickly scanned the space for Derek. Not seeing him, I moved further into the room, and that's when I saw her. Veronica was naked, strapped to a metal table, and she was bleeding from her right cheek and both of her wrists. I rushed over to her, checked for a pulse, and found a very slight one. I looked around the room, looking for something to wrap her wounds in until I could get her out. I was surprised to find gauze and medical tape in a cabinet not far from where she was restrained. Grabbing the supplies, I raced back over to her and dressed her wounds. Once I had her bandaged, I unbuckled her from the metal contraption she was bound to, and she collapsed into my arms. Hoisting her up over my shoulder, she felt paper-thin.

"Naomi, I'm coming out to you now. I have Veronica and she's badly injured," I screamed into the ear com.

"I'm coming, Neil. Where's Gina?" Naomi asked concerned.

"I'll come back for her, but we have to get Veronica out of here right now!" I answered impatiently.

"I'll be at the well in less than five!" she replied excitedly.

72

I ran down the hall with Veronica on my shoulder, praying that once I got outside the door, Naomi would be there. If she wasn't, I didn't think Veronica would survive. Bursting through the door, I said a prayer of thanks as I saw Naomi barrelling towards me in the Hummer. She pulled up in a screech. I ripped open the back door and laid Veronica down as gently as possible.

"Did you call Vince?" I asked hurriedly.

"Yes. They should be here in the next 15 minutes. He said he's going to bring out the force," she responded.

"Get her to the hospital now!" I yelled as I slammed the door and immediately ran back to the well door.

Naomi's voice came through the ear com, "Bring my best friend home, Neil!"

I sprinted down the tunnel from the well door. My heartbeat thundered in my ears as I said a silent prayer that I would find Porter alive. I couldn't lose her; not like I lost the others. I physically shook the thought from my head. I couldn't go back to Iraq, not now. Now, I had to make sure Porter was alive and hopefully kill Sparrow.

Entering into the area I'd found Veronica in, I kept my Sig sweeping in front of me, ready for anything. Adrenaline flooded my system as I cleared that room. Taking out the map I had drawn from Porter's intel, I looked to see how much ground I'd have to cover to locate her. There were two possible ways that Sparrow could have intercepted her once the alarm was activated. I stood in the middle hallway between the two passageways and decided to go left. The map indicated there were only four rooms in this direction, the other way had six. I would clear the left side first, and if I didn't locate Porter there, I knew I would find her on the other side.

The first two rooms were completely empty, and the third had random bits of furniture as well as a few boxes. The fourth room was filled with various boxes, barrels, and other leftover equipment from the factory's working days. Not finding Porter there, I ran to the doorway on the opposite side of the room that I had come in. There was another short hall that connected to the other side. I paused when I made it to the door, listened, and upon hearing nothing, I entered the room. The metallic smell of blood hit me immediately. My stomach knotted and my pulse quickened as I prayed the blood wasn't Porter's. Following the trail of blood to the other room, I saw evidence of a fight from the blood splatter on the walls as well as blood in several spots on the floor. *Where the hell is Porter?* my mind screamed as I feared I may be too late.

Going into the third room, I stopped when I heard a sound. I tilted my head trying to hear what had caught my attention. Stepping forward slowly, I realized the sound I heard was a moan. It came from behind a row of boxes on the right side of the room. I approached the boxes with my Sig ready, just in case this was a trap. Peeking around the boxes, my heart sank. Porter was balled up in the corner. Her right eye was completely swollen shut and it looked like her nose was broken. Blood covered her mouth and dripped rapidly from her chin onto her shirt.

"Neil," she coughed, blood flying from her lips, as she tried to raise her left hand.

I raced over to her. "Porter," was all I could manage to get out.

"Is all that concern in your eyes for me?" she whispered in an attempt to make a joke. Her breathing was jagged and laboured.

"Are you injured other than your face?" I asked.

"I think my ribs are broken, but I tased him before he could do any real damage," she explained weakly.

I lifted her arm to inspect the left side of her ribcage and that's when I saw the cause of her laboured breathing. There were several puncture wounds that seeped blood steadily. "Where is he now, Porter?" I asked, trying to assess if I could get her out of there without encountering Sparrow.

"I left him two rooms that way," she pointed toward the doorway behind me.

"I'm getting you out of here," I said, scooping her up in my arms.

"We've gotta stop him, Neil," she pleaded as she coughed up more blood. "Maybe I didn't tase him soon enough," she said as her head fell back and she lost consciousness.

Seeing her eyes close raised the level of fear that raced through me. "I'm not going to let you die on me, Porter. Vince should be here any minute. He can get that fucker," I said, even though Porter's broken face and body made my desire to kill him increase tenfold. I knew I couldn't handle it if another person I was supposed to protect died.

I hustled through the maze of rooms. I knew that Naomi was too far away for me to use the ear com to call for help. *Vince, where the fuck are you?* I thought as I made it to the entryway of the lab where Veronica had been, then everything went dark.

The darkness halted me in my tracks. The hairs on the back of my neck stood at attention. It didn't take my two tours in Iraq to let me know that this fight wasn't over. But with Porter in my arms, I knew I couldn't defend us. Remembering the layout of the room, I took a few more steps before putting her down on the floor. I slid the NV glasses down on my eyes and reached for my Sig. As my hand touch the butt of the pistol, I felt a piercing pain slash through my right shoulder blade, causing my entire arm to go instantly numb. I fell forward onto the floor. The NV glasses flew off and I was submerged into darkness again. Disoriented by my inability to see, I knew that if I didn't get up, he would stab me again. Suddenly, the room was bathed in red as emergency lights that must have been connected to a backup generator came on. I scrambled to turn over, just as he lunged at me. Seeing his attack this time, I was able to move out of the way of the blade, but not before it cut across my bicep. My adrenaline surged and I kicked out hard, connecting with his right forearm causing him to drop the knife. His face contorted in more rage than pain as he turned and rushed toward me. Prepared for his attack, I sidestepped and punched with my left hand, delivering a blow to his right temple. This time, he yelled in pain. I followed the punch up with a kick to his ribs as well as one to his right knee. Hollering, he went down.

I lifted my foot to stomp on his face when he reached out, grabbing the ankle of the leg that was planted on the ground and pulled. I went down hard; my head hit hard against the cement floor.

Immediately, he was on top of me punching my face. I felt my lip split. The taste of my own blood filled my mouth. Using a technique I learned in the military, I used my left arm to block his blows while bringing up my knees and kicking out. I felt his weight lift off of me and I knew if I didn't do something now, he would again have the advantage. Rolling to my side, I landed next to the KA-Bar I'd kicked from Derek. I grabbed the knife he'd dropped earlier and raised it just as he rushed me. We collided, falling over the same table Veronica had been strapped to, landing with a thud. He screamed. I felt his hot sticky blood cover my hand. The force of him hitting me along with the fall had caused the blade of the knife to penetrate his gut to the handle. His body went limp. I panted rapidly and pushed the weight of his body off of me and an alarm sounded somewhere in the room.

Struggling to my feet, I went back to Porter. Even though she was a tiny woman, with my injuries, it was difficult to pick her up. Fighting through the pain, I managed to get her over my shoulder because I was determined to get us out of there. It felt like I was in Iraq all over again which somehow gave me the strength to get through the tunnel and out of the well door.

As I stepped outside, the sounds of blaring sirens approaching quickly filled my ears. I staggered a few yards before the blood loss and pain caused me to stop and put Porter down. I collapsed next to her, as the first police car came into view. The car came to a screeching halt about 15 feet away and Vince jumped out before it fully stopped. He ran over to me, terror plastered across his face.

"Stamps! How badly are you hurt?" he asked as more officers arrived on the scene.

"Save Porter," was my answer as an ambulance pulled up next to us. The two EMTs inside jumped out and rushed over, one to Porter, one to me.

"Stamps, where's Sparrow?" Vince asked as the EMT started working on me.

"Inside," I said, wincing as the EMT touched the stab wound on my back. Vince immediately turned and began barking instructions to the growing number of officers on the scene.

"She has a collapsed lung, her BP is dropping, and she's lost consciousness! We need to transport her now!" the EMT working on Porter yelled.

"Go," I said pushing the arm of the man attending to me. "Save her!" I insisted. The last thing I remember was watching them load her into the back of the ambulance before it sped off.

Epilogue
Gina

I woke up in a hospital room with Naomi and Neil both asleep in chairs next to my bed. Neil's head was bandaged, and his right arm was in a sling. I tried to say something to let them know that I was awake, but my throat was so dry that nothing came out. One of the machines that were attached to me started beeping. The sound caused both Naomi and Neil to wake up with a start. They were both on their feet and at my bedside in seconds.

"G, you're awake! Thank God you're awake," Naomi said as relief spread over her face.

"Water," I managed to get out. Naomi quickly grabbed a cup from a portable table next to the bed. She held the straw to my lips and I took a long drink. "Do I look that bad? You both look terrified," I croaked.

Putting the cup back onto the table, Naomi looked at me intensely, "Don't you ever scare me like that again! You do not have permission to get yourself killed and you can't die again," she said seriously.

"I died?" I asked surprised. "What happened?"

"You had a punctured lung which caused your blood pressure to drop dangerously low. So low in fact that you were in cardiac arrest by the time they got you here to the hospital. They rushed you into surgery, and you died on the table, G. You died," she said, choking on the last sentence. "Thank God, they brought you back!"

"How long have I been here?"

"A week. You were in surgery for 10 hours. The doctors put you in a medically induced coma to allow your body to heal. Your nose was broken and a few of your teeth were knocked out. He broke four of your ribs, but they had to break three more during your surgery to repair your lung," Neil answered.

"Is Veronica alive?"

"She is, but it will be at least another month before she's able to leave the hospital. He did a lot of damage to her, and she has to have several reconstructive surgeries," Neil provided.

"Did we get him, Neil?" I questioned as the images of the encounter with Derek flashed through my mind.

His facial expression immediately changed. He stared down at the floor for a long moment before he answered, "He got away, Porter. I don't know how. I pushed that KA-Bar all the way to the handle. I heard him scream. His blood was all over my hand, but Vince said when they went in, they couldn't find him. They used our map, they searched every room, but they didn't find anything. They canvased the area 10 miles around the property, but it's like he just disappeared."

"They even went to his home and his job, and found nothing," Naomi added.

Their words hit me harder than any of the blows I had received during my fight with Derek. He was out there somewhere, and I had to find him. "Neil, we have to find him," I began.

"Gina, what are you talking about? He almost killed you! You *died*! Let the feds find this guy. You just need to worry about healing," Naomi said angrily.

"Veronica is probably never going to heal because of what he did to her. I can't ever feel safe knowing he could be out there waiting to hurt someone else," I informed her. "Naomi, I know that what happened scared you, but what if he does this again? What if he takes another girl, tortures and rapes her and this time he kills her? He's done it before and if we don't stop him, he *will* do it again!"

"I'm in," Neil stated.

"Damn it, Neil! Don't you start encouraging her! This is a ludicrous idea," Naomi pleaded as she shot daggers from her eyes at him.

"She's right, Naomi. He isn't going to stop. Someone has to take him down like the rabid dog he is, and I think I'm the man for the job. Besides, that fucker tried to kill me and my partner here," he said placing his unslung hand on my shoulder, "I owe him."

"Did you just call me your partner?" I asked, shocked by his words.

"Yes, I did. I figure once we're all healed up, we take a leave from the firm and take a 'vacation,'" he said, using air quotes. "Let's say we go big game hunting for a Sparrow," Neil said referring to Derek with a sly grin across his still bruised face.

"That sounds like a wonderful *vacation*," I said to Neil, using air quotes of my own. "You know I've always been good at finding monsters."

About the Author

There are many ways to describe Nubian Star, but none more poignant than the word driven! Nubian Star was born and raised in Milwaukee, WI. Early in her life, she had an affinity to the arts and words. Reading was a way to escape the hardships of growing up in Milwaukee's inner city. Throughout school, she utilized writing as a way to express herself. She was a four-time state medal winning member of her high school forensics team. Upon graduating high school, she entered the corporate workforce, but her passion for writing continued. She began performing spoken word poetry, where she competed in slams and toured the Midwest with the Rustbelt Team. During her time as a spoken word artist, she wrote two chapbooks, and co-facilitated a poetry workshop for youth at her local Boys & Girls Club.

A lover of all things art, Nubian Star began painting in 2006 and through this medium, she has used her art to influence her community. She received recognition from the Mayor of Milwaukee for her works in her neighbourhood. Her work in the community gave her an intimate view of how important creative work is in relation to healing. In an attempt to continue to use her artistic talents to help her community, she enrolled at Mt. Mary University as an Art Therapy major. While at the university, she has been a key member in several organizations as well as the community as a whole. She has been featured in several campus articles for her poetry and writing. Once she completes her degree, she will continue to utilize art and writing to heal her community and, hopefully, the world!

Nubian Star has also been a crocheter for over 20 years. She utilizes her love of yarn to create handcrafted works such as blankets, winter accessories, clothing, and intricate purses. Everything she creates is one of a kind pieces crafted with the specific intent of providing feelings of warmth, comfort, and love to those that wear her creations.

Writing has always been a major passion for Nubian Star and she thoroughly enjoys using her imagination to create intricately woven stories. A lover of writers such as Stephen King, Shel Silverstein, Nicholas Sansbury Smith, and Ntozake Shange, she uses her wide range of interest and knowledge to create mind binding works of fiction. A homebody, crafter, and domestic goddess extraordinaire, Nubian Star spends her free time enjoying the moments she creates with her family as she observes the world, waiting for the next strike of inspiration.

CPSIA information can be obtained
at www.ICGtesting.com
Printed in the USA
BVHW071014261122
652780BV00003B/604